ANNIE'S
High Sea Adventure

Adapted by Jill Max
Story and illustrations by Marek Mann

GEC GARRETT EDUCATIONAL CORPORATION

Annie loved boats.
Big boats, little boats, even boats in bottles.
She dreamed of an adventure on the high seas.

One day she set off along the beach.
Captain Cade had promised
to take her out to sea on his yellow fishing boat.
Annie could hardly wait.

She wondered if her friends Bobo and Dot
were going sailing too.

In the harbor seagulls circled overhead.
Captain Cade's big yellow fishing boat
was tied up to the dock.

"Anchors aweigh," shouted the Captain.
The big yellow boat sailed out into the sunset.

Annie looked back.
On the beach she saw Bobo and Dot
pushing their little red sailboat into the water.
"I'm off to sea," she called.
But they didn't hear her.

The lighthouse on the shore got
smaller and smaller.
The big yellow boat sailed
farther and farther away from land.
"Quick, haul in the nets," cried Captain Cade.
"There's a storm blowing up from the north."

Thick black clouds hid the moon and the stars.
The yellow fishing boat was
tossed and tumbled in the waves.

Suddenly, with a flash and a crack,
lightning lit the black sky.
"Look," cried Annie. "There's a tiny sailboat.
It's being swallowed up by the sea."

"Where?" Captain Cade shouted
above the noise of the storm.
Annie heard voices calling, "Help! Help!"
It was Bobo and Dot.
"Over there." She pointed. "Between the waves."

She guided the big yellow boat
toward the shipwrecked sailors.
Captain Cade pulled Bobo and
Dot out of the water.
"It's been a fine night
for fishing after all," he said.

"Annie, we were lucky to have you aboard,"
said Captain Cade.
"We were lucky you saw us," cried Bobo and Dot.
Annie felt lucky too.
She could hardly wait for her next
adventure on the high seas.

Edited by Elizabeth Bradford

U.S.A. text copyright © 1991
by Garrett Educational Corporation.
Originally published in Austria
by Mangold Verlag under the title
Urlaub am Meer
Copyright © 1990 by Mangold Verlag

Published by Garrett Educational Corporation
130 East 13th Street, Ada, Oklahoma 74820

Manufactured in the United States of America

Library of Congress Cataloging-in-Publication Data

Max, Jill.
  Annie's high sea adventure / adapted by Jill Max; story and
illustrations by Marek Mann.
    p.   cm. — (Magic mountain fables)
    Translation of: Urlaub am Meer.
    Summary: Annie and Captain Cade rescue Bobo and Dot
when a storm at sea capsizes their little red sailboat.
    ISBN 1-56074-027-2
    [1. Sea stories.]   I. Mann, Marek. Urlaub am Meer.   English.
II. Mann, Marek.   III. Title.   IV. Series.
PZ7.M44626Ar   1991
[E]—dc20   91-21305
                              CIP
                              AC